The Hired Man

A Musical

Book by
Melvyn Bragg

Music and lyrics by
Howard Goodall

30

Samuel French - London
New York - Toronto - Hollywood

ISBN 0 573 08071 2

THE HIRED MAN

First performed at the Nuffield Theatre, Southampton on 2nd February, 1984. Subsequently performed at the Leicester Haymarket Theatre on 19th July, 1984. First performed in London at the Astoria Theatre on 31st October, 1984; a Really Useful Company Presentation by Andrew Lloyd Webber of the Leicester Haymarket production. The cast was as follows:

John	Paul Clarkson
Emily	Julia Hills
Jackson	Richard Walsh
Ted Blacklock/Isaac	Billy Hartman
Seth	Gerard Doyle
Sally	Sarah Woollett
May	Clare Burt
Harry	Christopher Wild
Pennington/Vicar	Stephen Earle
Recruiting Officer/Dan	Craig Pinder
Jack/Union Chairman	Stephen Jameson
Landlady	Nelly Morrison
Joe Sharp	Gareth Snook
Bob/Alf	Robert Gill
Bill	Nick David
Ezra	Philip Childs
Josh	Tony Crean
Tom	Richard Bartlett
Beth	Janice Cramer
Hired Men, Farmers, Miners, Soldiers	

Directed by David Gilmore
Designed by Martin Johns

Period: early 1900s

MUSICAL NUMBERS

ACT I

1.	**Song of the Hired Men**	All
2.	**Fill It to the Top**	Isaac, Seth, John
3.	**Now For the First Time**	Emily, John
4.	**Song of the Hired Men** (Reprise)	All
5.	**Work Song: It's All Right For You**	Farmers, Men
6.	**Who Will You Marry Then?**	Emily, Sally
6a.	Interlude (Time Passing)	
7.	**Get Up and Go, Lad**	Isaac, Men
8.	**I Wouldn't Be the First**	Emily, Jackson
9.	**Fade Away**	John, Emily
10.	**Hear Your Voice (I)**	Jackson
11.	**What a Fool I've Been**	John
12.	**If I Could**	Emily
13.	**Song of the Hired Men** (Reprise) and Union	All

ACT II

14.	**You Never See the Sun**	May
14a.	Interlude (Jackson)	
15.	**What Would You Say to Your Son?**	John
16.	**Union Song: Men of Stone**	Seth, Blacklock, Men
16a.	Interlude (Gathering of Soldiers)	
17.	**Farewell Song**	Emily, John, Isaac, May, All
18.	**War Song: So Tell Your Children**	Isaac, Jackson, John, Emily, Men
18a.	Trumpet Solo	
18b.	Harp Solo	
19.	**Crossbridge Dance**	Isaac, All
20.	**No Choir of Angels**	Emily, John
20a.	**Hear Your Voice (II)**	Jackson
21.	**Re-hiring: Song of the Hired Men** (Reprise)	All

The Piano/Vocal Score and associated orchestral parts are available on hire from Samuel French Ltd.

SETTING

The settings for the London production of *The Hired Man* were ranged on two levels, with back projection used on the cyclorama. The cottage, when set up, became a permanent feature centre stage on the lower level, with events happening around and above it (as in the War sequence when the upper level represented the front lines with action going on above the cottage setting on the lower level).

The settings have merely been suggested in this Acting Edition. It should be stressed that a minimum of furniture and scenery should be used so that the action flows swiftly from one "scene" to the next.

The Hired Man

My paternal grandfather died in 1970. I would guess that he had never read a book in the twentieth century. He left school at the end of the nineteenth century when Queen Victoria sat securely on a vast Empire, rich and varied beyond belief. His part in it—like that of the great majority of people in this country—was humble; he worked. First on the land, where, like many farm labourers his exhausting working life was in some way relieved by his love for the horses he worked with and the landscape he saw every day. Then as a miner where close friendships gave some relief. Like so many others of his generation he was swept up into the First World War: unlike many others including some of his brothers—he survived it to come back to a land which promised nothing but more sweated labour. A few years after that war, his wife died leaving him with four children: he had four more by his second wife.

As my father was away in World War Two—I was born a month after it broke out—I might have seen, in my grandfather, someone who stood both for himself and for my own absent father. I was certainly close to him and despite his sternness and occasional flaring bad temper, I liked seeing him. I was the first in my family to stay on at school and when I went to university that both baffled and delighted him. I became a prize subject for teasing—an occupation he greatly enjoyed. When I began to publish novels he had a field day.

One day at the end of the sixties I went to see him and was shocked to realise that he knew he would die soon. He never said anything, of course. Nor did I: not about that. He complained a bit about his legs; not much, but the lack of mobility profoundly upset the order of a man who had measured out his life in physical effort. He said nothing at all about the arthritis crippling his hands. His pale blue eyes still teased away at my latest comical episode—joining the BBC this time. But I knew, without question, that he was going to die.

Afterwards I went for a long walk around the Cumbrian town in which I had been brought up—the town he had lived all my lifespan. I decided to write a book "about" him.

This turned into *The Hired Man*. Once the book started, then the few facts I knew about him were revealed as no more than a starting point. About his relationship with his first wife, to take just one example, I knew nothing: the description presented in *The Hired Man* is a total fiction. What remains is the outline of the facts of his life.

And the outline of the lives of tens, even hundreds of thousands of the people of this country in the first quarter of the twentieth century. What I wanted to do in the book was not only to present the personal story of the

sort of man whose life is so rarely written about, but also to chronicle and
bring alive that cavalcade of British history which swept us into a new
century and into a war to end wars.

My grandfather used to play the melodion—the working man's accor-
dion. He had a good voice: several of his children and grandchildren sang in
choirs—still do, some of them. He would have loved Howard Goodall's
music coming, as it does, out of that ancient English choral tradition which
has influenced so many of our best twentieth-century composers. It was the
music which persuaded me to let the book be turned into something else. I
had resisted its being filmed or televised or dramatized. This music,
though—apart from its own qualities—fills out the feelings and completes
many strong emotions unspoken in that walk of life. I wish that the old lad
could have lived to enjoy it.

Melvyn Bragg
27th June, 1984.

ACT I

SCENE 1

The Hiring

Song 1: Song of the Hired Men

Men   Hear us coming, O running, O drumming up our strength
Hiking, exciting and fighting o-ver the wages
None has a poorer lot than we
But they'll never O never O be as free
No they'll never no never be as fancy free
As a farmer's hired man
O to be a hired man

Hear us coming, O running, O drumming up our strength
Hiking, exciting and fighting o-ver the wages
None has a poorer lot than we
But they'll never O never O be as free
No they'll never no never be as fancy free
As a farmer's hired man
O to be a hired man

We're not hurried O flurried or worried for ourselves
Grinning, heads spinning not giving in o'er the beggars
Price on our labour though
There are others, our brothers who shy away
From the meagre pay other days we would agree
But today we're free hired men
O to be a hired man

Twice a year here we sell you ourselves
Cannot offer you anything else
'Tisn't dear we sell cheaply for a cottage and
Eighteen shillings
We are worth your shillings—is it done?
Throw me a luck penny will you, O
Show your intentions are that true, O
If it's done, yes it's done
Sure of it, sure of it
Sure?—then it's done!

Pennington Are you for hire?
John Ay, I'm for hire.
1st Farmer Are you for hire? I want an all-round fella: you'll have to work
in with everything.
1st Man But what horses do you have?
1st Farmer Clydesdales—and I want them looked after: the man who
wastes them gets his marchin' orders.
1st Man I've always liked working with horses best.
1st Farmer Maybe. How big's your family?
1st Man Six. There's a cottage goes with it, isn't there?
1st Farmer Don't rush, lad. I haven't made me mind up yet. There's a lot of
good muscle about today.
2nd Farmer You'd have to do man's work.
Woman I've never done anything else.
2nd Farmer Ay, but I've hard land, fell land; bitter work, lass.
Woman I've never been frightened of hard work.
2nd Farmer I'll think on it. I've always hired a man, see.
Woman I'm a lot cheaper; and I've no family to feed.
2nd Farmer I'll look about.
3rd Farmer Where were you last?
2nd Man Parton of Dean.
3rd Farmer Why did you leave?
2nd Man We had a difference.
3rd Farmer Oh ay.
2nd Man We fell out.
3rd Farmer What's your name?
2nd Man Joe Sharp.
3rd Farmer I want no troublemakers near me. On your way!
Men (*singing*)   We've been drinking we're stinking but living
                        Hear our thrilling and willing awakening walked for miles but
                        O! wouldn't miss a hiring
                        Blisters stinging, ears ringing, not suffering—
                        We're expecting a better life tomorrow
                        When we'll still be hired men
                        O to be a hired man.

                        Throw me a luck penny will you, O
                        Show your intentions are that true, O
                        Is it done, yes it's done
                        Sure of me, sure of you
                        Done?—to be sure!

4th Farmer What do you expect?
3rd Man Seventeen shillings a week.
4th Farmer Fifteen's my limit ... Will your wife help out?
3rd Man That depends.
4th Farmer We'll give you your vegetables.
2nd Farmer Fifteen and sixpence and dead meat.

4th Man One shilling for luck and it's done.
5th Farmer Done.
6th Farmer All right, lass. Ten shillings.
Woman Twelve?
6th Farmer Ten. And all found.
Woman I suppose it's the best I'll get.
6th Farmer Done.
Pennington Sixteen shillings all you'll get from me, lad.
John Eighteen.
Pennington Your wife'll get her vegetables.
John I'll hang on.
Pennington You'll do no better here today. I guarantee that.
John I'm not working for that.
Pennington I'll throw in some dead meat. That's my limit!

John (*singing*)   Two dozen others like me, or more,
Two dozen want the same job I'm in for
Two dozen heroes recruiting for a war with the land,
New shillings in their hands,
A bargain for such a man.

Show me your luck penny will you, O
Knowing I'll take any that's true, O
Look at me, bid for me,
Deal with me, hire me,
Call, and I'm yours.

I must be among the youngest
And rate among the strongest I'm
Married with a good wife though
Soon she'll need a midwife I'm sure,
Yes it's done!

John goes across to the waiting Pennington, spits on his own hand, shakes on the deal and takes Pennington's coin—the "luck penny"

Men   Here us coming O running O singing o-ver the fields
We till, more the work of gods than men
But we'll never, no never, regret the day
That we put ourselves willing in the hiring ring
O to be a hired man
O to be a hired man

Throw us your luck pennies will you, O
Show your intentions are that true, O
Are you sure, yes you're sure
Is it done? Yes it's done
O to be a hired man
O to be a hired man.

Isaac leans on the mine shaft

Isaac Is thou for hire, lad?

John (*embracing him*) Isaac!

Isaac What the hell, boy. I'm your brother not your mother. Keep yourself fresh for your wife.

John Are you hired yet?

Isaac Me? I have schemes John. One of which is on four legs with our Seth. First Commandment—don't give in until you're gaspin'! I'll only come to these miserable beggars if my luck goes bad. You know me, John; only work if you can't avoid it.

John I've taken Pennington's coin.

Isaac You can always give it back. Remember the Good Book—the lilies of the field, they strive not—but just you *look* at them blow! Be a lily of the field, John; like me: come and have a pie and a pint.

John Well, I think I'd better wait here . . . for Emily.

Isaac Come on, kidder—grab a bit of life!

Men   Throw us your luck pennies will you
            Show your intentions are that true O
            Are you sure, yes you're sure
            Is it done, yes it's done
            O to be a hired man
            O to be a hired man!

John and Isaac move into the "pub" area

The landlady comes on with a jug of beer

Seth enters with a whippet

Seth John!

John Seth!

They shake hands

Isaac The Tallentire boys.

John The Three Musketeers.

All All for one! . . . (*Looking at the whippet*) . . . And one on all fours!

Isaac (*to the Landlady*) Right, missis. Three pints and six meat pies. I'm in training!

Seth How's married life?

John You should give it a try yourself.

Isaac He can't . . . the dog won't let him look at another woman.

Seth It was a bit sudden wasn't it?

John These things happen.

Isaac Not to me they don't.

Seth Best of luck to you . . . you must have walked twenty miles to get here. What was wrong with home?

John Father.

Isaac Still behaving as if he owned the place, eh?

John Ay! And Emily wanted away. She got a lift in a pony and trap. She should be here any time now.

Seth Where'll you live?
John There's a cottage, he says, a bit run-down but I can have it.
Isaac You know what run down means don't you?
John No.
Isaac It means it used to have four walls.
Seth What did you get?
John Sixteen shillings.
Seth You'd get better wages down the pit with me.
John I want farm work.
Seth There's no future in it, John.
John Emily wouldn't suffer pit life.
Seth Needs must, John, when the devil drives.
John Emily's got a bit of devil in her, herself.
Seth We can use that.
John What for?
Seth We need to organize.
John Yes?
Seth If we're to keep going forward, John. It wasn't long ago we had
    women and children down those mines. Listen to this—(*he produces a
    paper "The Evidence of a Lancashire Woman 1842"*)—"I have a belt
    round my waist and a chain passing between my legs and I go on my
    hands and feet. The water comes up to my clog tops and I have seen it
    over my thighs. I have drawn till I have the skin off me . . ."
Isaac Come on, man, even the whippet's getting depressed!
Seth Give up this farm work. Come with me.
Isaac Leave him alone. He's a wife to look out for and a life of his own to
    lead. Let him be. John wants farm work. Beats me—but so did our father.
    So did our grandfather. It's a Tallentire family tradition!
Seth What happened to you, then?
Isaac I've got another tradition.
Seth Drink, dogs and wrestling.
Isaac Ay, it's a straight line down from our grandmother.
Seth Show some respect for the dead.
Isaac She's not dead, she's just having a rest before her next bout.
John Ay and you'd better get some of this down you before yours . . .

Song 2: Fill It to the Top

Isaac   I propose a toast to life
      To sport, good fun and ease
      A life of risks, of dice and chance
      I give you all of these!
      Farm work means you're stuck in one place
      Mining's worse—underground at the coal face
      Fill it to the top man,
      Get it down
      Pass another round
      Then I'll drink to that!

Isaac sits

Seth   I will drink to a better life
For all our working men,
A living wage, a good old age
To that I'll say amen
Justice—we can fight for that John
Progress we've deserved for so long
Come and work the mines, lad
Leave the land
You'll soon understand
That's where happiness lies!

John   I will toast the best of all
The girl I did this for
Our life together, and soon a child
I couldn't ask for more.

All   Good health, here's to two young lovers
The baby on the way and his two fine brothers
Fill it to the top man
Get it down
Pass another round
Then we'll have some more,
Fill it to the top man
Get it down
Pass another round
That's what toasts are for!

Pause

Emily enters

John (*going to meet her*) There she is. Emily! Emily!
Emily John!

They embrace

We are going to stay a bit and look around, aren't we?
John Ay, there's a fair here. I've got myself hired. (*He puts her on top of the mine entrance*)
Emily I knew you would. Whereabout?
John Crossbridge. Eight miles. It's up in the hills.
Emily I could do with the walk after sitting on that blessed cart all morning. And *talk*. He could deafen a donkey. He went on and on.
John Isaac and Seth are here. I was quite pleased to tell you the truth. I know nobody else.
Emily That's what I like! Don't you see? Oh, John.

Song 3: Now For the First Time

(*Singing*)   Now for the first time we're out on our own
Taking for once our decisions alone
We'll have a home and some wages to share

No-one will know us from Adam up there
People won't ask why we married so young
Won't disapprove of the things we have done

Say farewell to the idle suspicion
We don't need permission to
Say farewell to the shaking of heads
At the two newly-weds
But when I say "I do" then I do
Yes and I say I do I love you.

Two unknown faces, we've only ourselves
Taking our chance somewhere high in the fells
I'm not ashamed we decided to leave
I'm not afraid of the reasons that we've got to

John
Emily }

Say farewell to our fathers and mothers
And all of those others who
Said farewell thinking "they'll soon return"
Saying "they'll have to learn
That to think for yourself is a crime",
And it may be their view but not mine:
Say farewell to the whispers and winks
And a village that thinks that we'll
Ne'er do well but we'll prove that they're wrong
And it won't be too long before
They wish that they'd done it too
And be sorry they didn't have you!

They kiss, John lifts Emily down. Isaac and Seth approach

John There's Seth and Isaac now. Come and say hello.
Emily How do I look?
John All right. This is the brother you didn't meet. Seth. This is Emily.
Seth Sorry I couldn't make the wedding, missis. The very best of luck.
Emily Thank you for the knives and forks.

They shake hands

I appreciated them. Hello Isaac.
Isaac Am I welcome, missis?
Emily My mother still hasn't forgiven you for setting up that cock fight half way through our wedding.
Isaac As the prophet says—"When you see a chance for a bit of sport, drop everything".
Emily He would be shown the door in our house—prophet or no prophet.
John (*of Seth's whippet*) Is that thing any good?
Isaac Oh yes. Oh indeed it is. It can fly, John. I've seen it. It's got my shirt on it today. That bitch'll have been well fed and exercised. It'll have been well looked after. I just hope that John treats you as well as Seth treats this bitch of his, missis.

Emily Thank you, Isaac.

Seth I'd better walk her round a bit. Can't let her stiffen up. (*To the whippet*) Come on.

Seth exits DL *with the dog*

Isaac Right! Let's see if we can drum up some sport.

Emily Is it bear-baiting or just a fight to the death?

Isaac Wrestling.

Emily Well, I'll hold the bucket for the blood.

Isaac (*taking off his jacket*) You've married a joker there, John.

John Take no notice.

Isaac I never do, John. I'll watch you, young lady. Right then! Who'll take us on. One fall. Sudden Death. Cumberland and Westmorland style. Five shillings. Five shillings here in my hand!

Jackson Hold on to these, Father. (*He hands Pennington his jacket etc.*) I'll wrestle you!

Isaac Good man. There's my stake.

Jackson And mine!

Pennington More money than sense.

Isaac There always is, mister. Have we a judge? Dan?

Dan Right.

Isaac May the best man win.

Jackson Jackson Pennington.

Isaac Isaac Tallentire. You've a good grip on you.

The men get into the grip for Cumberland and Westmorland wrestling—arms over and under, hands locked over opponent's back, posture crabwise, aim to break the other's grip by throwing him. Shouts of "Come on, Isaac", "Come on Jackson" etc. After a strong tussle—strength (Isaac) against litheness and cleverness (Jackson)—Isaac wins. Jackson's father has thrown down his (Jackson's) clothes. Jackson goes to pick them up. John has gone to congratulate Isaac. Emily is on her own

Emily You should have won.

Jackson He's like a bullock.

Emily But you were a lot faster. I think you should have won.

Jackson smiles; a moment

Isaac and Seth exit

John (*not seeing Emily with Jackson, calling unanxiously*) Emily.

After the wrestling, music as everyone begins to move off, John and Emily to the cottage

Song 4: Song of the Hired Men (Reprise)

All   Hear us going, o'erflowing, not knowing where
        Though we're tired, we're hired, we've fire in our hearts
        Tied by a luck penny only
        Bargained for more money vainly

O to be a hired man
Give our whole lives to the land
O to give our hired hands.

Hear us going ... (*Fading into the distance*)

The chorus is repeated until the stage is clear, as all exit

In the cottage:

John Well, we've started out.

Black-out

SCENE 2

Work

Song 5: Work Song: It's All Right For You

All	From dawn till dusk each hour
	Each day each week
	The whole year
	No waking moment can we waste here
Farmers	From head to toe each limb
	Each bone each muscle
	Straining
	We'll not have idling or
	Complaining.
Men	It's all right for you though
	You have men in your employ
	You're all right 'cos you know
	Such good men in your employ!
Pennington	From cot to grave the land's
	No slave it craves
	Attention
	The day of rest is man's
	Invention.
Farmers	Anchored in the hard earth
	You'll survive through sweat and toil!
Men	What would grow without us,
	Who would tend this barren soil?
	If we were you though, we'd be the same
Men (*singing*)	When things went wrong we too
	Would shift the blame!
All	Though like our forefathers
	We're poor men
	We've still the strength of those that
	Bore them

And pray our children are such proud men,
Proud men.
If you lived our lives you'd be the same
In your hearts too would burn such a flame.

In the cottage:

Sally You know I didn't have anyone to visit 'til you came here.

Emily I'm not surprised in a place like this.

Sally The minute I saw you and John at Cockermouth Hiring, I knew we'd be best friends. Is Crossbridge what you expected?

Emily It's too much like the place I came from for comfort. Same farm talk; same sleet; same blessed rain on washing day.

Sally People like thee. And you've made a marvellous job of this pigsty Pennington foisted off on thee.

Emily I nearly went mad when I first saw it. And John would have turned round and gone home if I'd let him.

Sally Everybody says what a good worker he is.

Emily Good? Hard, you mean. He does nothing else. He seems to lose himself in it. He has no time for anything but that blessed work.

Sally But you're married, and there's May; what more does you want?

Emily I thought we were starting out on something, not finishing up with something.

Sally Emily Tallentire, you do love him?

Emily Yes . . . of course . . . don't be silly.

John (*singing*) No snow too deep no fell too steep will e'er
Defeat me
I'll never rest from work completely

All It's all right for us though
The open air's our second home

John No greater pleasure than work done well
Against all weathers high on some fell
No finer sight than ploughed furrows deep
To eek out ripe land from hillsides steep.

Pennington Here's your dinner. Save you coming up to the house.

Jackson And keep our noses in it, eh, Father? Considering the age of that bloody plough, John has fair claim to be a miracle worker.

Pennington Language. Have you finished that bottom field, Jackson?

Jackson Half an hour since.

Pennington You work too fast. I'll go down and see what you've missed.

Jackson I'm off for a pint. John?

Pennington He can't afford to drink.

Jackson Not on the money you give him.

Pennington You'll go too far one of these days.

Jackson You can put money on that, Father. Have my tea, John.

Jackson exits L

Pennington Slow work.

John That field can't have been touched for a century.

Pennington I never had anybody I thought could handle it.
John I enjoyed doing it. I like seeing it all opened up like that. You'll need a new plough.
Pennington Chance'd be a fine thing. My father had five men working with him. I've you.
John And Jackson.
Pennington Work's the only thing that's cheap today. I've got no money for new ploughs. All we've got is toil, John.
All Come lend a hand come give your all come spare
Your whole life
Come take the strain come use your
Whole might

The Men turn to face the Farmers, and the Farmers turn to face the Men

Men It's all right for you squire
You have men who'll break their backs
It's all right when you tire
You've got us to take the slack
Counter Melody We work until we drop, work until we die.
If we were you, though, we'd be the same
Farmers But you are not!
Men When things went wrong we too would shift the blame
Farmers It's all right for you men
Make the best of what you've got
The fact of the matter is this men
We're in charge and you are not

Counter Melody We work until we drop, work until we die.
All The fact of the matter is this then
You're/we're in charge and
We/you are not!

Black-out

SCENE 3

Crossbridge

In the cottage, Sally and Emily are folding sheets

Sally When I get married it'll be perfection or I'll go back home.
Emily Ah, we'll see.
Sally Except nobody'll ever ask me.
Emily You are a bit past it. What is it, seventeen?

Song 6: Who Will You Marry Then?

(*Singing*) Who will you marry then, who will it be?
When they come courting you will you agree?

	Who'll be your beau when you go to a dance? Will you encourage or check his advance? How about Josh with the short curly hair, Didn't you once go with him to a fair?
Sally	Don't say him! He's a nice enough lad but I'm scared of his dad and he's Far too thin— Nothing firm to hold on to if he were upon you I won't say "I do" not to him.
Emily	Who will you marry then who will you take, Who will adore all the cakes that you bake? Will it be Tom with the long hairless legs, Whiter and brighter than newly-laid eggs?
Sally	Don't say him! Don't say Joe from the pub who is shaped like a tub And don't say Jim Who breeds dogs for a hobby he's worse than our Bobby No I don't think I'd do just for Jim. He will be simply the best I can find He will be handsome and clever and kind
Emily	Someone with looks, lots of books and a heart? Sally that isn't a promising start!
Sally	I will have someone who's blue-eyed and tall I will have *Jackson* the best of them all! I'll have him! He's a wonderful man I'll wed him if I can
Emily	Marry him? Sally such a good match is the hardest to catch
Both	If he *did* say "I do" then he'd do If he *did* say "I do" then he'd do!

They finish folding the sheets and put them in the basket as they talk

Emily Have you proposed yet?
Sally It'll come to that.
Emily He likes you.
Sally That's the trouble. I could be his bloomin' sister for all he really cares. I'll have to run back. Thanks for helping with the sheets. (*She takes the basket and sheets*)
Emily Tomorrow?
Sally Tomorrow. (*She leaves the cottage and meets:*)

Jackson as he enters

Pause

Jackson Hello Sally.
Sally Jackson. What are you doing down here?
Jackson A bit of peace and quiet.
Sally Oh. Well then. I have to go. See thee.
Jackson See thee.

Sally exits

Pause

Anybody home? There's a fine day out here—waiting to be used up.

Emily comes out

Emily Do you just take a day off whenever you have the mind?
Jackson Ay. More or less. I won't be round here much longer. (*He goes up on the rocks*)
Emily You fancy yourself, Jackson Pennington, don't you? (*She moves to the upper level*)
Jackson Just as well somebody does.
Emily Oh—Sally thinks you're the sun and the moon.
Jackson Sally's a very nice kid. Sally was the best thing around here until *you* turned up.
Emily Sally's got plans for you.
Jackson Has she now? Fancy one? (*He offers her a cigarette*)
Emily Well . . . can I try a puff?
Jackson Very good.
Emily I could get use to it . . . You've been all over the place, haven't you?
Jackson Here and there.
Emily Where would you really like to go—if you could choose anywhere at all?
Jackson I've thought of Australia or Canada. I'm not sure I wouldn't get just as restless there. You take yourself with you wherever you go, don't you? I can't get it out of my mind that there has to be more to life than this—not just the work here or the same face, some of that has a pull, it's kept me at the end of its rope so far—I mean more to it than what I've done, I suppose, then what I've added up to. I keep thinking—that can't be all there is, it just can't be. But maybe I needn't go far now. Maybe what I want is home.
Emily I can't see anything to keep you here.
Jackson Thou can't or thou won't?
Emily Same thing.
Jackson Show us your left hand. (*He takes Emily's hand*) I can read palms, you know. I'll tell you what you'll do.
Emily Jackson.
Jackson I'll keep the bad bits to myself.
Emily I think I'd better go. (*She rises and takes her hand away*)

Jackson rises. They are very close

Jackson Are you afraid of what people would think?
Emily You can't be too careful in a place like this, can you, Jackson?

Jackson stays and watches as Emily goes into the house

Black-out

6a: Interlude: Time Passing

SCENE 4

The Hunt

In the cottage:

Isaac enters with his bag

Isaac By crikey it's wet! Hello all. Too wet to knock. Sorry, missis. By God if it knows anything at all up here it knows how to rain!

Emily Sit down and get dry—let me take your jacket—you'll have something to eat—John!

John Come and have a chair.

Isaac Well. (*After a pause*) I should have let you know, missis; I know I should.

Emily You'er welcome any time. Sit down.

John I heard you were cutting granite down at Moota.

Isaac I was, then a butcher took us on and then I helped a fella sell a few horses and one way and another I've got money for a few weeks, do-as-I-feel-like.

Emily Dost thou like apple pie?

Isaac I do, Emily, I do. You've found a weakness there. But—I'd better say what I have to say first, missis, thank you all the same. Can I light up?

Emily Of course.

Isaac (*lighting his pipe*) There's those that take offence. Now then: This Melbreak pack is having a hell of a season, and my plan is to follow them for a month or two.

Emily I didn't know you had a horse, Isaac. Didst thou win it?

Isaac It's not your low country style hunting here missis, is it John? It's all on your own two feet in these hills: just us lads running after a fox with a few dogs, but what sport!

John I've seen them up on Blake sometimes.

Isaac Nothing finer ever invented. But what I need is what you might call a *basis* like. Not for every night. If fox takes off I'll stop where we drop. But what I want is somewhere to leave my things for a few weeks. I'll pay for my feed, of course: I'll insist. As the prophet said: "If you can't pay—don't stay". And I can sleep on that mat in front of the fire there—best bed in the house.

Emily Of course you can stay . . . And—why don't you take John with you? He's never given himself a single holiday. He used to have so much "go" in him, Isaac.

John That was before I had responsibilities.

Emily Only ones you make for yourself. We're stuck here. Sometimes I think my head'll blow off. We do nothing.

John We went to see your mother last Christmas.

Emily Oh John!

Isaac He's like our mother, missis, work-worms. She'll have a pinny on when she meets St Peter and ask him if there's any scrubbing out to be done.

Emily Go on, John. Pennington owes you time off.
John It'll have to be thought about, Emily.
Isaac Now I didn't come here to split up a family.
Emily It would do him good, wouldn't it, Isaac?

Isaac wanders over to the table and takes the whole of the apple pie

Isaac Good? I don't know about good, missis. Good's a very tricky article. But—he'll have a hell of a time! He'll be with lads who know about sport and hounds that can sniff up a scent on a stone road—and we'll be after that fox, missis, the best little creature there is—the animal that can run rings around two dozen men and a pack of hounds and then have time to sit and tidy up his tail—he'll be *hunting*, missis, that's what he'll be doing, eh John? What do you say, kidder—have some sport!

During the song, Isaac and John move to the "pub" and are joined by the other men

Song 7: Get Up and Go, Lad

(*Singing*)
You don't want to be locked up
You don't want to be tied down
You don't want to be left out
You need to look around and try your luck
No matter what they say to you
Don't be shy
For if you stop to ponder life will
Pass you by,
Left high and dry
No matter what the risk might be,
It's better to be fancy free,
Try O try!

Get up and go, lad
You're looking so sad
Soon you'll be so glad you came along,
Your blood'll run round
And make your lungs pound
And when the sun's down
We'll have a hair of the dog
And sing a hunting song!

All	Ha!
Isaac	Up there—an unknown fell
All	Ha!
Isaac	Stone walls and frozen ground
All	Ha!
Isaac	See there—a glimpse of fox
All	Ha!
Isaac	And all around the sound of baying hounds
	Tumble trip and gallop down a

Rolling scree
We leap another thirty fences
Blind to all the consequences—
Follow me!

Isaac goes to the upper level

All   Get up and go, lad
It isn't so bad
To play nomad for just a while
You've not had fun yet
You've not made one bet
Come see a sunset
Where we will drink the blood o' the fox
And make you smile!

Isaac (*speaking*) I give you a toast lads: to Mister Fox—God bless him! And
the life of Riley—God bless that!

John I thought we'd lost him in Holme Wood—I thought we'd never get
him out!

Isaac They're going into Lorton tomorrow. Fancy another day? We shall
have to sleep here.

John (*singing*)   If I should hunt an extra day
I fear what Emily might say
The bed half empty,
And she'll sleep lonely,
But what of my own desires?

Landlady   Men who roam, your wives at home
Won't miss you while you're gone . . .

Back home in the cottage:

Emily (*singing*)   Love why are you turning.
Love where are you leading us?
Now he seems a weaker man
I wish I could understand

I know that it's also me
That I want to see
A man he cannot be
These nights when I lie awake
When I cry awake
He too is still awake . . .
Wide awake . . .

In the Pub:

John (*singing*)   I've not spent nights away before
Or been off work a day or more . . .

To hell with worries,
I'll take my chances,

I'll choose for myself this time—
Enjoying myself's no crime.

(*Speaking*) Yes! I'll send word to Emily with Joe Sharp. Yes. I won't do it
again will I, not for a long time? One more day.

Landlady	Men who roam, you're far from home,
	Your wives are fast asleep . . .
All	Ha!
Isaac	You don't want to be locked up
All	Ha!
Isaac	You don't want to be tied down
All	Ha!
Isaac	You don't want to miss the sport
All	Ha!

Isaac tours the group of men

Isaac	You don't want to tow the line—
	Do what you ought.
	No matter what your wives mean to you
	Stay O stay!
	And even if you miss them they won't
	Go astray,
	They're here always
	I'll wager you'll be glad you stayed
	I'll bet you're here for one more day
	Cast care away!
Wenches	So stop your qualing
Men	So stop your qualing
Wenches	Join your wassailing
Men	Join your wassailing
Wenches	Let's get some ale in—
All	And then you'll stay!
Men	You'll set a fast pace
Wenches	You'll set a fast pace
Men	With your new found taste
Wenches	With your new found taste
Men	And at the last race
All	You'll find your life the final price
	You have to pay,
	You'll find your life the final price
	You have—to—pay! Ha!

Black-out

SCENE 5

After the Hunt

In the cottage, the table is laid for supper

Jackson It's a fine welcome that.

Emily I've asked you to keep away.

Jackson Yes, it's a fine spread.

Emily He's a fine man.

Jackson He must be.

Emily He'll be back soon. With Isaac.

Jackson No, no they won't ... Joe Sharp brought word they're stopping over for another night.

Emily Oh ... so that's why you've come down here.

Jackson I can't stop wanting you, Emily.

Song 8: I Wouldn't Be the First

Emily	I wouldn't be the first
	Nor would I be the last
	You'd want me for a time
	Until your passion passed
Jackson	We've been through all this before
	There are no others any more
	There's only you, only you
Emily	Suddenly, you're not the man that
	Countless girls pursued
	Suddenly, you change your ways to
	Suit my fickle mood
	I have everything to lose
	And it's me that has to choose
	And pay the price, I pay the price.
Jackson	Come away
	There is nothing for us here
	All that holds you back is fear
	You must break free
	Come away
	I'd have long since gone by now
	But for you I don't know how
	I could have stayed
Emily	Let me be
	You know I want to go
	You know I feel the same
	But still my answer's no
	Still I can't abandon John
	Still I feel our love is wrong
	I cannot go, I cannot go
Jackson	Suddenly you think of him
	Despite all you have done

Emily	Suddenly I think of him *Because* of what I've done
	I could not leave Though inside I want you so Though with every hour I know I want you more I could not leave, In his way John cares for me In my heart I'd not be free From what has been.
Jackson	Say this won't last Our love has passed Say you don't love me.
Emily	You must go Though all you say is true If I let you stay I'm scared of what I'll do If I could I'd come away If there wasn't John or May It cannot change, it cannot change
Jackson	Tell me why you have to stay Tell me love won't find a way Tell me you don't love me
Emily	In the end I can see myself reach back And it isn't that it lack The strength to move I cannot leave Though inside I want you so Though with every hour I know I want you more, I want you more …
Jackson	I know you want me, Come let me hold you Come give your love, come give your love …

They embrace. Jackson exits. The music climaxes and continues under:

John and Isaac are near the cottage

Isaac I'll hunt a few more days, John. Expect me when you see me.

John We'll do it again, won't we?

Isaac Won't we just. You're a dab hand at it, John. You were up and down those fells like a rabbit in a lather.

John You're a lucky old devil.

Isaac Correct.

John When you see Seth, tell him to drop in again soon. Emily likes talking to him.

Isaac He's a terrible serious man for talk. Still, that whippet has made me a bob or two in its time.

John When will we see you again?

Isaac When my feet run out.

John So long then.

Isaac Regards to Emily and May and look after yourself, kidder. *Away.*

Isaac exits

John moves to the cottage

John Emily . . . Did you get the message?

Emily Yes. I did.

John It was such good sport.

Emily I didn't mind you going. You sounded like Isaac then. "Such good sport."

John Isaac was the lad! You should have seen him.

Emily What did he do?

John Oh . . . just about everything. He was the life and soul of it!

Emily Come on then, John; give us all the crack.

Pause

John How's May then?

Emily Fine. Grand. She's no trouble at all.

John Anybody drop in?

Emily No. Nobody at all.

John Except Joe Sharp?

Emily Joe Sharp?

John With word. That I was staying over.

Emily I didn't mind you staying over.

John I wanted to get back.

Emily You could have had another day or two. You've earned them.

John Maybe I will then. Next time.

Song 9: Fade Away

(*Singing*)   Once she told me everything
                        Now she'll not say anything
                        Once she was in love with me
                        Now she seems uneasy

                        Can't say what I want to say
                        What I mean to say
                        What I never say
                        Don't know what she thinks of me
                        What I'm meant to be
                        Will I ever see.
                        There behind those sad eyes
                        There I know the answer lies . . .

Emily   Cold my touch unsettles him
                        Cold wraps round our feelings
                        Love which once had tenderness

Now is dull and passionless
Our love must it fade away, has it more to say, did it
   mean to stay?
Our live will it nqt awake for our future's sake, or will it
   steal away,
Steal away ...

Black-out

SCENE 6

The Pub—The Fight

Jackson Right lads, drinks on me.

All cheer

Tom We wouldn't be here if they weren't.

They all laugh

No, no. I'm only joking. Last time you will be here with us like this. Once
people been in the Army, they've never the same after. Look at my uncle
Geoff, joined the Army, came back: completely changed.
Dan How?
Tom Dead.
Josh You make sure you don't get yourself killed.
Jackson I'll do my best.
Bob I wouldn't mind the getting killed, it's the discipline I couldn't stand.
Fifty lashes if you so much as break wind.
Dan Sounds just like home to me.

General mirth

Josh You'll miss home, though, won't you, Jackson?
Jackson What's there to miss?
Tom Well, the ale.
1st Man And the girls. Eh, Jackson.
Josh Now none of that. Arh, I remember when we were lads, I wasn't half
soft on this girl, and when I asked her if she'd kiss me she said, no, she was
saving herself for Jackson Pennington.
Jackson No.
1st Man Ay, and you remember that day at school when they found that
cow pat in your desk?
Jackson How could I forget.
1st Man That was me!
Jackson It wasn't.
1st Man Ay. It was. Revenge. Reckoned she'd not go kissing a man who
kept cow pats in his desk. I didn't half have trouble sneaking it into school
though. Had to put it in with my dinner things. Sandwiches that day,
worst I ever had.

Dan Sounds just like home.

Great mirth. Dan is very pleased at the reaction

2nd Man Did they hold your (*he gestures*) and make you cough?

The Landlady turns away delicately

Jackson They did.

2nd Man I wouldn't trust mine to anybody.

3rd Man I doubt if you could get rid of yours a rummage sale.

2nd Man Well, what happened when you coughed?

Jackson He said "You've got a good set of lungs, young man".

2nd Man What? They baffle me, doctors.

Tom Where do you think you'll go to, Jackson?

Jackson I think I'll apply for India, sun all day, elephants and Maharajas. All that fightin' and the North-west Frontier. And all those dancing girls.

Dan Sounds just like home.

Josh No, but it's no joke, is it? Couldn't bring myself to do the killing. "Thou shalt not kill." How do you feel about that, Jackson? Are you prepared to kill a man?

Jackson Wouldn't be going if I wasn't. What's a rifle for?

John and Isaac enter

Jackson John, Isaac, it's on me.

Isaac Very handsome of you, Jackson.

John Thanks.

Isaac What are we celebrating?

Jackson I'm off to the Army.

Isaac No.

John Bit sudden.

Jackson You know me, John. Do a thing first, think about it after.

John It's a big decision though, good luck.

Isaac Brings it back, this, doesn't it, Jack? Your twenty-first. You remember that?

Jackson Ay.

Isaac When all those gypsies came to town.

Jackson Ay.

Isaac You've never seen such a thing. The drinking, the dancing. The Vicar near died of shock: but they gave us a good time, didn't they?

Jackson Ay, they did.

Isaac Of course, when we woke up in the morning they'd gone and stolen everything.

Man The hens.

Josh The lambs.

Tom The women. Oh no, sorry about that, Bob.

Bob No, that's all right. Never you mind, that's fine.

Josh She was always a wild one.

Man You're better off without her.

Bob Ay.

Tom And now you've got your dog, haven't you?
Bob Ay.
Tom More reliable.
Bob Ay. You don't get a dog dancing and putting on ear-rings and spraying on lots of perfume and running off with the gippos.
Tom No.
Man It would be a bloody funny dog if you did.

Joe Sharp enters. He whispers to Jackson

Dan I've a mind to join the Army. Do they let you take your wife with you?
Jackson No.
Dan Even better.
Jackson Put another round in, missis, I'll be back in a minute. (*He goes outside the "pub"*)
Isaac I tell you what we've just seen on the way up here. A pack of weasels. Has anybody seen them packing?
Man My father has.
Isaac Frightenin'. I've only seen it once before. I was sleepin' out—it was good dry weather—and down they came. And what a sound they make. It was like something out of the plagues of Egypt.

Cut to Jackson outside the pub, alone. Music. The Lights dim in the pub

Song 10: Hear Your Voice (I)

Jackson   Hear your voice, calling me
                 See your eyes, facing me
                 Dream of you in my sleep

                 But you're not there, Emily
                 Life with you can never be
                 Our two bodies never meet.

                 A last goodbye,
                 Then I'll take my leave and go
                 Though tonight for once I know
                 You would be mine,
                 You would be mine . . .

Emily meets him

Emily So you weren't going to come and tell me at all.
Jackson I would've told you.
Emily No. You were going to get drunk tonight and slink off tomorrow without even seeing me. You must have known I would hear about it. You're the talk of Crossbridge, Jackson, going for the Army. Biggest thing that's happened for months.
Jackson We had our chance.
Emily It's over for you, isn't it?
Jackson There's no point in this, Emily.

Emily Just a few months ago you would run over a fell just to spend five minutes together. Just a few weeks ago you would make sure you knew every move I made.

Jackson And what did you do? You told me about May, you told me about John—you held on and you held on. Look where it got us.

Emily Don't go.

Cut back to the Pub. The Lights increase

1st Man Where's Jackson got himself to?

2nd Man What was it you told him, Joe?

Joe Sharp Never you mind. Bring them in, missis.

Isaac Joe's a regular postman, aren't you, Joe?

John Owe you a drink for that.

Joe Sharp No trouble.

John No, no, now. You brought word back from Lorton to Emily. Fair's fair. It gave me another day's hunting.

1st Man Ay, but you passed it on to Jackson, didn't you, Joe? It was Jackson delivered the message to Emily, wasn't it?

Joe Sharp Be quiet!

John Jackson!

Song 11: What a Fool I've Been

(*Singing*) The furtive looks and timid glances
Now I see what they were
And though I sensed that she was restless,
Still I trusted in her.
Her distance, her silence,
It all meant the same . . .

And not a soul would tell me plainly
Not a friend said a word
Their secret kept by all who knew me
Not a whisper I heard.

Their distance, their silence,
They all knew the truth . . .

During the song, John leaves the "pub" and meets up with Jackson

And what a fool I've been
Didn't recognize the signs
Didn't guess the countless times
They must have shared
They must have shared.
And what a fool I've been
Didn't read it in her eyes
Didn't hear the endless lies
There must have been
There must have been

What did I do that made our love die,
And that took her from me?
No force on earth would make her love me
If she had to be free
But I cared, and I shared
The best that I had . . .

And what a fool I've been
Didn't recognize the signs
Didn't guess the countless times
They must have shared
They must have shared.

And what a fool I've been
Didn't read it in her eyes
Didn't hear the endless lies
There must have been
There must have been.

John Jackson!
Emily John. Leave us alone. Please.

The fight. Jackson is felled

Song 12: If I Could

Emily   If I could
I'd catch them as they fall
Sheild them from the pain
And heed them when they call
Both deserved much more than this
For them both I would have wished
Another love,
Another love.

Suddenly, before my eyes
My darkest fears come true
Suddenly, I know that there is
Nothing I can do.

What went wrong
That an anger so extreme
One that nothing could redeem
Was brought to life?

Now I know
I should have been aware.
That you would make this move
That only you would dare
Though I knew it had to end

With your love I could pretend
You wouldn't go
You wouldn't go

But suddenly, you think of me as
Someone else's wife
Suddenly, I'm just another
Chapter in your life

Was I wrong?
When I chose at first to stay
Thought it broke my heart each day
I had no choice.

You saw my tears
You shared those fears
Why must you go now?

How they stare
Witness to my shame
And though I made no move
It's me that gets the blame
"It was her that led him on
It was her that wasn't strong
She didn't care
She didn't care"

So pass me by
And let me cry
Tears that would ask me,

Emily
Is it love
That was left me here
    alone
That has robbed me of
    my home
And told me lies?

Is it love

Or a pain I once en-
    dured
One that nothing could
    have cured
And never dies

And never dies
And never dies

John
All we had
All the hopes we

Brought with us here
Are at an end.

Our dreams are gone
Wounds that life itself
Couldn't heal

Wounds that tear our
    love
Apart
And never die.

Jackson
There's nothing here
    now
Nothing to hold me

Without your love

And though I leave
    here
I'll never forget love

Forever strong

A flame that burns

Forever bright.

Emily	Love that nothing could have cured And never dies . . .

Song 13: Song of the Hired Man (Reprise)

Hired Men	Hear us coming O running O Drumming up our strength Hiking, exciting and fighting O Hear us coming O running O Drumming up our strength Hiking, exciting and fighting O Hear us . . . etc
Miners	Men of stone, your wives at home Your future's in our hands.
All	Step by step and pit by pit We'll find the promised land

CURTAIN

ACT II

May and Harry

It is early summer 1914 in Crossbridge

The scene opens to the sound of birds, countryside. A shot is fired

May How can you run on a day like this?

Harry (*ignoring her*) He must be in that wood over there.

May If you go any nearer he'll shoot you ...

Harry I want to see his gun.

May Then where will we be? Mam'd kill me: Getting you dead. Especially here.

May sits on a rock

Harry I'll just go over and see.

May Suit yourself. I'm sure I'm not moving from here until that sun stops being so bloomin' sweaty. (*She begins to take off one of her Edwardian garments*)

Harry May!

May Yes?

Harry What if folk see?

May See what?

Harry Well ... you.

May I think I'm very nice: I don't mind showing myself off.

Harry They can be funny in a place like this.

May (*still undressing*) What do you know about a bloomin' place like this?

Harry Are you sure I was born here?

May Almost. I certainly was. I think I can remember it.

Harry Will it be all right if I leave you?

May It will be better than that. Go and get shot. (*She stretches back voluptuously*) I'm going to give myself up to pleasure——

Harry Oh May!

May —worship the sun!

Harry Shut up, will you? Somebody might be listening.

May Go away, little brother, and leave our big sister to the Forces of Nature.

Harry Sometimes, May, I think you should not be let out.

Harry exits R

Song 14: You Never See the Sun

May
You never see the sun come out in our town
You never see a gap between the clouds
I'd be happy in a place like this
Now I see what I have always missed.

Here, the only things that move are the trees
Here, the heather reaches up to my knees
Here, I might meet a handsome country lad
He might be very hard to please ...
Should I be so scantily clad?

I never want to see another town again
Never want to wake up to the rain
We could move back to the cottage down there
Go to dances and have straw in our hair.

Oh, I wish I could have seen this before
Oh, nothing could have suited me more
Here, I could stay and sun myself to sleep
Yes now I see what summer's for
If only there were slightly less sheep.

She puts her hands in sheep's droppings

Here, the village lads swim bare in the brook
Oh, I wonder if they'd mind if I look?
Here, lovers come a'courting and court in the hay,
I wonder what they really do
If only they'd include me too.

Jackson enters. He has a gun and three dead rabbits

Jackson Somebody's cheerful.
May Oh ... I'm sorry. (*She struggles into her clothes*)
Jackson Sorry?
May No, I mean, well ... so it was you.
Jackson Was it?
May Shooting. My brother's looking for you.
Jackson Has he got a gun?
May No.
Jackson I'm relieved to hear it.
May But he loves guns. Just like a boy.
Jackson Oh, I see. Are you here for a day out?
May Yes, but I was born here.
Jackson Were you now.
May In that cottage over there, I think.
Jackson Oh yes.
May Nearly sixteen years ago.

Jackson (*after a pause*) Yes. You'll just be a couple of years ahead of the century. Well now. What's your name?

May May Tallentire.

Jackson That's right. Yes.

May Maybe you knew my father and mother?

Jackson I could well have done . . .

May He's down in the pit now. In Whitehaven. The seams go out under the sea there, you know.

Jackson I had heard.

May I wish he'd stop. I wish he'd come back somewhere like here.

Jackson And . . . your mother . . . your mother?

May Oh, she's all right. Do you live around here?

Jackson I used to. I come back now and then.

May Harry went over to that wood. He'll be mad because I talked to you and he didn't.

Jackson Would Harry like a go with the gun?

May Would you let him?

Jackson Yes.

May Would you really?

Jackson Yes, really.

May Cross your heart and hope to die? . . . no, don't do it, it's unlucky. Look. Stay here. Stay exactly where you are. Don't move and I'll bring him back. You won't move will you?

Jackson I won't move.

May It'll make his day you see. Because he didn't really want to come. He only did it, well, to please me in the end although don't you tell him that. He won't admit to that . . .

May exits

14a. Music Interlude

Jackson sits. He smiles, takes out tobacco, rolls up a cigarette. The Lights slowly fade on him

Black-out

SCENE 2

Whitehaven

John is on stage in an easy chair

Emily enters R

John Hello.

Emily Hello luv, you're up.

John It's too bright to sleep.

Emily I got some pie; you eat so little . . . (*She moves to the table*) May

should've been here to lay the table. She has a fancy man, you know. I'm
sure of it.

John I'll have an hour or two at the allotment.

Emily There's that meeting.

John I pulled up a couple of lettuce when I come past this morning. They're
out back.

Emily Oh. Thank you.

John I meant o tell you but you were in such a rush for your work.

Emily Mr Carrick gets very nasty if we're late.

John I fail to see why you want to work at all.

Emily I like it.

John Nobody likes work.

Emily Thou used to.

John I was younger and dafter then. Why do it when you don't have to?

Emily There's over two dozen women down at Bobbin Factory now.

John Single women.

Emily Three married.

John Not to me. May's working. Harry's going to start up this very week.
It's not a family, it's a factory you've got here.

Emily Please don't start up, John. As long as I can cope, let me work. My
money gets us nice trips out, doesn't it?

May enters

May Hello, everybody!

John Ah. Trouble.

May (*sitting with John*) Harry's on his way. Mrs Edwards says Wednesday;
is that all right? She wouldn't say any more. A man from Maryport
bought two coats in one go today, he said they were both for his wife but
they were the same coat and he asked me to wrap them up separately—
waste of paper I said but he insisted—very suspicious we thought and why
does he come all the way from Maryport in the first place . . .?

John Perhaps he thought he had a bargain at a cheap shop like yours.

May Cheap yourself! "Robson and Robson" is just the very smartest ladies
outfitters in all West Cumberland. Suppliers to the Quality we are.

John That cuts us out.

May Dad. Don't start again.

Emily May, there's a lettuce out the back. Run and fetch it.

May Oh, lettuce, lovely. (*She gets the lettuce*)

Harry enters and sits at the table

Harry What's to eat? I'm famished!

Emily Harry!

John We could always kill a sheep.

Emily It's on the table.

Harry Is that all there is?

Emily There's a pie, lettuce, tomatoes, bread, butter, cheese and tea. Yes.
Pretend it's a picnic.

Harry I like something hot.

May Go outside and fry yourself on the pavement.

John "I like something hot." You sound just like your grandfather. If he didn't have two hot meals a day he thought the world was caving in.

Emily He's still growing.

May I wish he'd stop: he's looking more like a garden rake every day.

Harry Better than having hair like string.

May Dad!

John Harry.

Harry Mam?

Emily Just eat up ...

There is a clatter of knives as they all eat

Mr Forrester says he can see you on Thursday. All being well you should get a start in a week or two.

May I started the Monday after I left school. The Monday after the Friday. He's had nearly two weeks' holiday already.

John It's not so easy to get work outside the pits.

May Why does our Harry have to be let off going down the pits?

John Because his mother doesn't want him to end up like me.

May I can understand that. But he needn't need he?

Emily Your father should never have left the land.

John There's no money in it. But Forrester pays well enough at those stables.

Emily He's always been good to you.

Harry I don't want to work with horses. I want down the pit.

Emily Just finish what's on your plate.

May Wish I'd had a choice.

John Your mother's decided.

Harry But I was never asked, was I? I was told.

May So was I.

Harry All you want is clothes and lads so you keep out of it.

May Dad!

Emily Harry! You're not going down the pit. I don't know how ever you can think about it after the Wellington. Just ... burnt. (*She goes to the fire*)

John Your mother's right. It's no life.

Harry I'll feel soft if I don't.

Emily I'm not having it. It's bad enough with your father. Every time that siren goes it turns me over.

John It's filthy work altogether, Harry. You're on your back in a two-foot seam or up to your thighs in water. You're worrying about gas or props.

Emily It's worse being under the sea.

May I can never understand why it just doesn't fall in on top of you. I mean, there's a lot of sea, isn't there?

Emily May!

Harry The money's good. All my mates are down there. And there's you, Uncle Seth, Uncle Tom, most of us.

Emily And most of them would give their eye-teeth to be out of it.

Harry It's getting better, though, isn't it? After the Wellington, Uncle Seth's helping everybody to get better conditions.

Emily Nothing'll stop it being dangerous work, Harry.

John Look at me. I came home this morning, lovely bright day and I had to go to bed. Next week's shift, I'll set off in the sunshine and waste the day at the bottom of that blooming shaft. Believe me, Harry, it's far nicer to work on top of the ground.

Harry I went to see Mr Stephens this afternoon. I'm starting on Monday.

Emily Harry!

John I thought as much.

Emily Well your father'll see Mr Stephens and tell him you *won't* be starting on Monday.

Harry You wouldn't do that, would you Dad?

Song 15: What Would You Say to Your Son?

John
What would you say to your son
If you were me?
Would you want him to go down there
And try to agree?
Would you tell the truth
When he asked for proof
Of the danger

What would you want for your son
If you were me?
Would you put him down a mine shaft
Under the sea?
Would you fill his breath
With a dust like death
Would you take him
Under?
Under ...

Would you cage him till you break him
And condemn him to the black rock?
Cage him till you break him
And condemn him to the black rock?
Would you say that to your own son
If you were me?
Would you allow him his own choice
Would he be free?
Would you shake your head
After all you'd said
Knowing he'd go
Under,
Under ...

Down there where there's no air
And you're locked up with the black rock
Down there where there's no air
And you're locked up with the black rock.

What would yo say to your son
If you were me?

Black-out

SCENE 3

The Union Meeting

Song 16: Men of Stone

Seth   Every man here has a grievance
Every man needs some allegiance
Every man seeks to improve the miner's lot
Every man speaks with defiance
Every man longs for some guidance
Every man must join the Union like it or not!

As each new member joins, our power grows
With every new reform more lives are saved

If anyone won't join the Union
If anyone holds that opinion
We'll tell him we won't have his labour in our pit

Men of stone, your wives at home,
Your future's in our hands
Strength to strength with bold intent
The Union's well-knit band.

Blacklock Hey-up lads, the preacher's in his pulpit! Watch your language.
Chairman Order now please, Ted. Let's get it started. I've told you
before...
Blacklock And I've told you an' all. We've come here to talk about the
hewers. I haven't all night to waste on his daft Union patter. I want you
lot off my back!
Seth So that you can work in with the owners and do the other lads down?
That's no way, Blacklock.
Blacklock One more word. You've plagued me for long enough.
Chairman Order now. Order! Or you'll have to leave the meeting.

Pause

I declare this meeting open.
Blacklock Right!

Chairman Sit down Ted. We have other business first. Sit down or I'll close it down.

Blacklock reluctantly sits

Secretary and treasurer's report taken as read ... all agreed?
Men Agreed.
Chairman Carried ... Now, as you all know, we've had a number of complaints. Seth Tallentire here's been asked to talk about the Union and show how useful it is. Complaints first ... not yours Ted ... we'll come to that in a minute.

Seth (*singing*)   Tell us your bones of contention
                    Show us your claims for a pension
                    Bring us complaints of conditions underground
Seth and   Men of stone, your voices grown,
supporter   Across the nation span
or two   Town by town a standard found
                    The Union's guiding hand!

1st Miner The pumps in the fire pit haven't been working for over a fortnight. We're up to our bellies in water some days. What's the Union doing about that?
2nd Miner We've heard about those inspections after explosions, and that's all that happened ... hearing about it ... what's the Union doing about that?
Seth We can answer all these complaints—and as many more—when we're strong enough. We have to be strong first.
Blacklock Not if I can help it!
3rd Miner They promised to give us more pit props but we still haven't enough.
Blacklock The more they spend on timber for props the less there is for us.
Seth Safety before profits.
  (*singing*)   With every new reform more lives are saved
                    We'll get you real compensation for widows someday
                    And we'll demand timber pit props whatever they say

Seth and Supporters	**Blacklock and Supporters**
Men of stone, your wives at home	Do you think that will fool us Everyone knows it's nonsense.
Your future's in our hands.	No-one here needs your endless rules and
Strength to strength with bold intent	Restrictions spoiling everything.
Across the nation span	If we take your advice we'll find we're left behind
	And end up poorer still.

Blacklock Cloud bloody cuckoo land, I've got kids talk more sense. You'll all end up like a lot of sheep—but not me. It's this eight-hour day I'm here for—it's no good for anybody. The hewers in Durham won't have it ... neither are we ... what's the point of leaving a good seam when you're into money? I've come here to get it stopped and I'd like to see the man who'll argue against it.

Seth I'll argue against it.

Blacklock You've said more than enough already. Sit down and shut up.

Seth It's the owners have sent you, isn't it? They'll use you and then just throw you over when you've done their dirty work. Why are you taken in? Come along with us, man, and fight for your rights.

Blacklock I can do my own fighting without hiding behind any Union of his.

Seth You hide behind the bosses instead. Why else do you get the easiest seams all the time? Everybody knows. Because you suck up to them. You're too frightened of them Ted.

Blacklock Take that back.

Chairman Now lads, now then. Order.

Blacklock Take that back or I'll ram your teeth down your neck.

Chairman Order!

The fight

Seth and Supporters	**Blacklock and Supporters**
Men of stone won't walk alone	Do you think that will fool us,
Your fellows by your side	Everyone knows it's nonsense
All your virtues, all your pride	No-one here needs your endless
The Union magnifies	rules and
	Restrictions spoiling everything.
	If we take your advice we'll find
	we're left behind
	And end up poorer still.

Blacklock and his supporters exit

Seth   Every man sworn to the Union
             Every boy born in the Union
             Every child knows that it's where their future lies
             Every pit pledged to the Union
             Every vote cast for the Union
             Not a man toil in the mines that won't comply

All   Soon every man will hold a Union card
             Soon every pit will bear a Union flag
             Soon every town soon every city will be
             Proud to say with all their heart:
             We're Union men!

Black-out

SCENE 4

Before the War

In the kitchen, May and Emily are packing John's things for his departure

Emily Come on now May. You'll do no good carrying on like that.

May I can't help it. I'm useless about crying. I always have been.
Emily You must hold up. Think of your father.
May I do! But every time I think about him I want to cry, and I think about him all the bloomin' time.
Emily May! Now stop it, or you'll set me off, then where will we be. We can't let him down. Now then. Can we?

Pause

Good. Well done. Now then ... have we got everything?
May I packed that new pair of socks for a surprise. Do you think he will like them?
Emily I'm sure he will. (*About to shut the suitcase*) We're ready.
May Just a minute. (*She looks around, goes to an old teapot or vase and takes out a bag*) Bullseyes!
Emily Won't they get very sticky?
May They're his favourites. He always takes them down the pit with him.
Emily (*picking up a piece of coarse brown paper*) Come on then. (*She wraps the bag in the paper*)
May They won't sell them in France you see.
Emily Likely not.

Harry bursts in

Harry You should see them! Come and see them. Dad and Uncle Isaac and Uncle Seth and everybody! Come on! Let me carry that. Come on! There's a band and everything.

He grabs the case and rushes out. May rushes after him. Emily follows

16a: Music Interlude

The Recruiting Officer and Men enter

Recruiting Officer Now then men. Because you are men. The King's Men. Fit to be. Proud of it. Men I say. Now then. You are here. I say that. Here you are. Today. Taken the King's shilling they used to say. Tradition. That's the Army. That's why we're here. All of you. What I say is. *Good.* You've volunteered. You could have stayed, some of you, in jobs. Down the mines. Good easy jobs. But you've volunteered. And that's why we'll beat the Hun. See. All of you. And because of that. Christmas ... you'll be back. Here, with your families. The Army has a heart. Remember that. Now then. We leave in two minutes. Attention. Dismissed.

Song 17: Farewell Song

Emily What a handsome man you are in uniform
If the weather stays like this you'll be too warm
Take this heather to remember me by
Fight your battles but come home alive.
John Oh, Emily there's no need for tears
Oh, listen to their passionate cheers

| | Hush, I'll be back before the winter's out |

Isaac and the rest:

Hush, I'll be back before the winter's out
You'll not spend Christmas on your own
I'll always think of you here at home.

Isaac   There's no need to worry lass we'll soon be home
Seth and I'll take good care he's not alone

May   Do us proud Dad, we expect you to win
Send a postcard when you get to Berlin!

Emily   Oh I'll miss you Seth look after him well
Oh I love to hear the tales that you'll tell

(To John)   Say when you're home we'll go back to the land
We'll start again just like before
And go back to the place we began . . .

Farewells

John   Oh, every precious letter I'll keep
Oh, at night your words will soothe me to sleep
Love, promise that you'll pray for me each day
And even though I'm far away
I'll always think of you here at home.

All   Oh, lovers shed your last precious tears
Stay, listen to their fearless young cheers
Hush, tiptoe past their final, fond embrace
'Cos after all you never know
When you'll next be seeing that smile.

Oh, lovers shed your last precious tears
Stay, listen to their fearless young cheers
Hush, tiptoe past their final fond embrace
'Cos after all you never know
When you next will see that smile
When you next will see that smile.

The Lights fade to Black-out. Gunfire

SCENE 5

The War

Song 18: War Song

Isaac   My clothes are wet, the trenches stink
My boots are worn, I have to limp
When weather's bad the dug-outs flood
And no-man's-land's a pool of blood.

Soldier   The mud here's worse than I've ever seen
We lost last Friday a boy of sixteen

	We can't advance and we will not retreat
	So we'll wait here until next year
	When we'll more or less still be here.
All Men	We sweat, we drink, we curse
	We survive here
	Don't stop to think who's next
	To save a friend we'll risk our necks

Out in no-man's-land
Who will come for us then?
Will they wait till dark
Will they leave us for dead?

	And far away our sons asleep
	Dream glorious dreams
	To them we're brave
	To them we sing
	Magnificent themes
Isaac	Last night our Tom from Maryport
	Untimely had his life cut short
	We found his corpse without a face
	But his evening rum won't go to waste
Jackson	The guns were pounding all through the night
	I cannot sleep 'cos the rats will bite
	Even the bravest men shake with fright
	But we'll hold fast, we'll be steadfast
	Till the war has passed us all by
All Men	We swear, we sing, we kill
	And we die here
	Don't like to think ahead
	Don't care to contemplate the dead

In the kitchen:

Emily (*singing*)	Though I'm proud of you
	John don't take any risks
	Scared and trembling I read the causality lists

In the trenches

Jackson (*speaking*) Isaac? Isaac? It's me—Jackson.
Isaac My leg. They've took my leg.
Jackson Hold on.
Isaac Keep your head down.
Jackson I'll carry you.
Isaac I'll be too heavy for you.
Jackson Put your arm over my shoulder and bite on that. It's a bit of wood.
Isaac You'll never make it, lad.
Jackson Bite hard.
Isaac Leave us till dark. Get help then.

Jackson You won't last. Come on.
Soldier (*singing*)   They gas us out and we have to run
                              We gas them back so they don't stay long
                              They lay some wire before an attack
                              We open fire so they can't get back
John   You'll have heard about Isaac losing his leg
                              They say without Jackson's help he'd be dead
                              We can't shift the Hun and the Hun can't shift us
                              So we'll stand firm while the tide turns
                              And the final German is dead.

                              Dear Emily
                              Remember me to both my children
                              Dear Emily
                              I hope there'll never be
                              Another time like this one.

In the kitchen:

Emily (*writing a letter*) What can I tell him, May?
May You can say our Harry's doing well down the pit.
Emily He is. He likes it there. Maybe it's worked out for the best. They won't call him up—that's one worry less.
May Dad says he likes to hear about how we're all doing. Just ordinary things, he said, didn't he?
Emily That's true. But it all seems so petty when you know what he's doing.
May Maybe you could tell him about Aunty Sarah running off . . .
Emily That would make your father laugh.
May Do you think he ever gets those parcels we send?
Emily He'll tell you when he does get them, don't worry. Run along with those letters to your Aunty Peg. I must set Harry's supper out, and I want to finish this first.
All Men (*singing*) We crawl, we climb, we cry
                              We're expendable
                              Don't care to count the cost
                              Ten men or more last night were lost.

                              Out in no-man's-land
                              Who will come for us then?
                              Will they wait till dark?
                              Will they leave us for dead?

                              So tell your children all one day
                              Of our sacrifice
                              Tell them we died young, our work undone
                              Tell them pride has its price.

In the kitchen:

   Isaac enters

Emily Oh, Isaac!
Isaac Now then, now then ...

Pause

Isaac I'm fine Emily, I'm fine. Calm yourself Emily, I'm fine. Wrestlin's out, I'm sorry to say. I tried it in the hospital in Kent but I stood on a fella's foot so hard I broke his big toe. Nice young fella he was an' all. From Newcastle. But I'll be hunting again!
Emily Hunting!
Isaac You dangle your stump in a bowl of vinegar every night and it's surprising how soon it toughens up. Oh ... it'll be no bother.
Emily Have some tea. Harry'll be home soon—he'll want to see you.
Isaac No ... I've my own home to go to, but I promised a man I'd come and see you before I saw anybody. A man I couldn't break a promise to. It was Jackson Pennington, Emily, bravest man you could hope to meet.
Emily Oh.
Isaac Yes—he said he didn't want to write a letter ... I suppose he thought letters can lead to trouble, but, he wanted to be remembered to you. That was the word.
Emily I see ...
Isaac I've since heard he's dead.
Emily Oh God. You know I made a fool of myself over him once. I don't think John's ever known how much I care for him ever since.
Isaac When I saw John last he was bearing up well.
Emily How is he? Does he look well? What's it really like there?
Isaac Like? ... *Like* ... nothing on earth, missis nothing.
All Men (*singing*)   We crawl, we climb, we cry
                                        We're expendable
                                        Don't care to count the cost
                                        Ten men or more last night were lost.

                                        Out in no-man's-land
                                        Who will come for us then?
                                        Will they wait till dark
                                        Will they leave us for dead?

                                        So tell your children all one day
                                        Of our sacrifice
                                        Tell them we died young, our work undone
                                        Tell them pride has its price

In the kitchen:

Emily Oh no.
Harry I signed up.
Emily Oh no. You're too young, you're just seventeen.
Harry They took me for eighteen and a half.
Emily I could go and tell them your real age.
Harry You couldn't do that ... You wouldn't do that, Mother.

Emily Oh, you shouldn't go.
Harry I can't not.
Emily Live while you can. Wait the extra year.
Harry It'll be over by then.
Emily So it's just the killing you want.
Harry No ... But I can't not, that's all.

They embrace

Emily I'll miss you.
Harry I'll send all my wages straight back.
Emily (*singing*)   What would you say to your son if you were me?
                         Would you allow him his own choice,
                         Would he be free?
                         Would you shake your head, after all you'd said,
                         Knowing he'd go over ... over ...

                         Out there, in the burnt air,
                         Where they're cut down to the black rock?
Seth   Some of the other men think it's all wrong
                         I've heard officers say it's gone on too long
                         They said it would end by the end of the year
                         They must be short of volunteers

                         They said we'd have won by the end of the year
                         But no-one has gained but the profiteers
                         I can't see the sense when so many must die
                         We're not all right, they're not all wrong,
                         Both say God's on our side!

                         Some blind, some maimed, some mad
                         Few survive this
                         Young lads, their dreams all gone
                         One fate, one grave, one farewell song:
                         So you're proud of us ...
                         And reward us with this!
                         And our epitaph ...
                         On the casualty lists!
All   So tell your children all one day
                         Of this sacrifice
                         Tell them all our young, their lives unsung,
                         Were succoured with lies.

                         So tell your children all one day
                         Of our sacrifice
                         Tell them we died young, our lives unsung
                         Tell them pride has its price!

The music ends

John (*at the front*) They told me that Harry was the most willing lad they ever had. The captain himself told me that when I went over. He'd been out after a sniper. It was a brave thing to do. Poor lad. At least, they said, it was quick. They gave me some letters from you he was carrying on him; I'll bring them back to you, now that it's all over.

Black-out

Music 18a: Trumpet Solo

SCENE 6

Crossbridge Club Walk

The villagers line up for a group photograph

Photographer Everybody smile please, say cheese.

Vicar Welcome one and all to Crossbridge Friendly Society's Annual Day in this year of our Lord nineteen hundred and twenty. Since eighteen hundred and eight the Friendly Society has helped the needy of this Parish and today we celebrate its achievements in sports and music, in games and dancing. A celebration made more poignant because this will be the last of such days. The world has moved on and the Friendly Society finds itself no longer needed. Sic transit gloria mundi. Let us give thanks to God for what we have today and ask him to make us worthy of his Bounty. Amen.

All Amen.

John Glad we came up?

Emily It was a good idea.

John You needed something to take you out of yourself.

Emily Lovely, isn't it?

Vicar Welcome, welcome.

John
Emily } (*together*) Thank you.

Vicar You're newcomers to Crossbridge I take it.

John Well, no, not exactly.

Vicar I do hope I can persuade you to take part in some of the events we have organized.

John Yes, I've a mind to enter that ploughing contest—(*to Emily*)—what do you think?

Emily You should. You were good at it.

Vicar That's the idea.

John I think I've lost my tack.

Vicar Yes, yes, of course you will. Come along, follow me . . .

The Vicar exits

John Are you coming Emily?

Emily No. You go . . . I'll walk about.

John Right! You'll be all right?

Emily Good luck with the ploughing. (*She is cheered by his enthusiasm*) I expect you to win.

John (*grinning*) We'll see what we can manage.

John follows the Vicar off

May comes across to her mother

May So you've got here at last. I though you were never going to make it. In fact I thought you didn't want to come at all.

Pause

It must have been wonderful living here. Dad and his horses. He's always going on about that.

Emily He's off with the Vicar to try his luck in the ploughing contest. Run across and watch. He'd be tickled by a bit of attention.

Sally comes up to Emily

Sally It *is* Emily, isn't it?

Emily Sally Edmondson.

Sally Sally Wrangham these past fifteen years.

Emily How are you?

Sally First rate.

Emily Well. What a lovely surprise.

Sally It can't be much of a surprise. I've been stuck in Crossbridge all my life—I don't suppose I'll ever get away from it now.

Emily And what's the gossip?

Sally Oh—it's been nothing but Club Walk, Club Walk and Club Walk for weeks. Some of them wish this wasn't the last one. I'll be glad when they're over. It turns everything upside down.

Emily And what's new?

Sally Things have changed a lot since the war. Half the shops are gone. And men gone. Seventeen. From a little place like this. I was sorry to hear about Harry.

Emily (*after a pause*) They said it was quick.

The Vicar enters

Sally Mine were too young ... Thank God.

Vicar Ah, ladies, if you're very sprightly you'll just have time to get to the white tent in time to hear me declare the winner of the Baking Competition. Although if Old Granny Glossop's carroway seed cake doesn't take first prize this year as it has for the last fifteen, then I'm a Chinaman.

The Vicar exits

Sally
Emily } (*together*) Granny Glossop!! After all these years.

Sally Nothing like the old faces is there? It's the best part of it ... seeing the old faces again.

18b: Musical Interlude

John Why'd you give up betting, then?

Isaac The wife, John, the better half. Now I've got this butchin' business she says I need a bit of respectability. She was frightened I would bet my credit away—she has a head for money, I'll give her that. Well, how about a look at that scything contest . . . can't do much worse than you did with that plough.

John I was rusty.

Isaac I've seen a straighter line on a dog's back leg. If it'd been work you'd have licked it. You were never much at sport, were you?

Seth enters

John Is that Seth?

Isaac (*sadly*) Seth's an altered man since he went in for that Pacifist business. He just keeps his dogs as pets now. Pets!

John He's a good man. Seth!

Seth John! Isaac! Not a bad day for it.

John They were saying it's the last there'll be.

Seth That's why I came. Sad you know. I don't like to see these things going. Even though we're replacing them with better. There was a good spirit about some of these Friendly Societies. There was something like a family about them.

Isaac The day you stop dreaming, Seth, pigs'll smoke cigars.

Seth Is Emily here?

John Somewhere about.

Seth I hope you're looking after her now, John. She's priceless, you know. No other woman with her sense.

Isaac I suppose that means she supports you! Eh man, you're still a comic. Now, I'm going to see a man about a dog.

The Vicar returns and starts to organize the dancing

May (*to a young man*) Can you dance?

Young Man I won second prize at Crossbridge last Christmas.

May Come on then, sweep me off my feet.

Terpsichorean Break

Song 19: Crossbridge Dance

Isaac   So join the whirling
You should be swirling
Your partners twirling across the floor
Your life unfurls in
This hurly-burlying
Come boy and girling
From head to toe tomorrow morning
Will be sore!

All   Strike up the band lads

Wake up the grandads
Put on your gladrags
Get off your seat!
No don't just look on
Put your new boots on
You can't put a foot wrong
Believe you me you'll find
Life's better with a beat,
Believe you me you'll find . . .
Life's better on your feet!

The Dancers disperse, as Emily and John come away together. All applaud

Emily Oh . . . are we too old for this, John?
John Not a bit . . . we just need more practise, that's all.
Emily Why don't you go back to farm work, John?
John I was just thinking that! The very thought.
Emily Well?
John The money's still hopeless. I want nothing—except for you—you to
be well. That would do me.
Emily Oh, John. I haven't done enough for you.
John You couldn't have been better. No. I wasn't anything like lively
enough for you, was I . . . that was the trouble, wasn't it?

Song 20: No Choir of Angels

(*Singing*)   I gave no strength, no life to you
                         When we were first in love
                         You wanted joy, I gave you none
                         My work seemed quite enough.
Emily   You weren't to blame, John, I was wrong
                         I looked for love elsewhere
                         When you were hurt I turned away,
                         Was blind to your despair.
John   But Emily we were so young
                         Not everything was so undone
                         If only we had had more time
                         We've realized our love so late
                         Aware of how few real mistakes
                         Now perhaps we'll let it shine.
Emily   So we survived and here we are
                         Surrounded by the night
                         No choir of angels, no guiding star
                         Just our reflecting eyes

                         And this reminds me of when we met
                         Our whole lives still to run
                         Though we've both changed, our hopes subdued
                         Not all those dreams are gone

	But now I know the truth inside
	Now I know our love's survived
	Now I know will never die
Both	And even now it's not too late
	Our future we can still reshape
	And cherish what was once denied
Emily	If I had my life once more
	Of one thing I'd be twice as sure
	It's you that I would share it with.

Black-out

SCENE 7

The Pit

Miners come on to the stage and make their way to the pit shafts

In Emily's kitchen:

John You'll try to eat this now, won't you?

Emily Please don't do all that, John. It's me who should be looking after you.

John May'll be coming in about seven before she goes to work. She'll see to anything else you want.

Emily I'll be all right.

John You should've gone into hospital when the doctor said.

Emily I'm having nothing to do with hospitals, John. Please don't go on. You'll be late for work.

John Ay. Is there anything else I can get you? An orange? I'll peel it for you.

Emily I'm fine. I can peel my own orange!

John Right ... (*He puts on his scarf, picks up his tin, puts on his cap, looks down at her*) Now eat that up. (*He goes outside*)

Emily John!

John (*from outside*) Yes?

Emily See you later.

John See you then.

The Pit

Are we still on Derwent Seam?

Joe Just.

John We'll miss it.

Alec We'll miss it. It comes out like butter.

Tom How's Emily?

John Not so good. Not so good.

In Emily's kitchen:

Emily goes to the sideboard where she gets out a photograph. She looks at the photograph

The Pit—a two-minute break

Was that your lad I saw you with yesterday?
Alec Where?
John In Wilson's.
Alec Yes.
John By God, he's shot up.
Alec Eats like ten.
John You never know till they're out in the world.
Alec I won't grieve much to see the back of mine. They've been more trouble than enough. Mind—I wouldn't admit that.
John I see that Archie's lad's in bother again. Drink?
Alec And he'll only be half-fed in that house. Just like his father.
John Right, let's have another go at her.

First murmurings of the rush

Listen.
Tom What is it? Sounds like the sea.
John Sssh.

A low, distant rumble

(*Calmly*) It's rushed. Now then, lads: edge back ... very carefully ... just edge back ...

Black-out

The Pit Surface

The klaxon sounds for the accident

Man 1 It's rushed. Number Seven's cut off. They're out of Siddack.
Seth Number Seven. That's our John.
Man 2 There's three of them down there. It's blocked right back.
Seth We'll have to cut in through Moorbanks.
Man 2 It doesn't reach far enough. It could take two days.
Seth We'll make a new shaft. Somebody get word to their familes. Come on.

In the kitchen:

Emily Go and see, will you, love?
May They'll come and tell us ... *he'll* hardly be down there yet, will he? I want to stay here.
Emily It'll just take you a minute, I can knock on the wall and Mrs Graham'll come round if I need anything.
May Can't I ...
Emily Just for me. I'll want to know straight away, you see. Please.

In the Pit:

Tom (*scrambling along*) I'm going back. I'm digging through. The sea'll cave in on us.

Alec Steady on lad.

John Tom! You'll bring it all down. Get hold of yourself.

Alec John's right, lad.

Tom I can't stop thinking about the sea . . . up there . . . miles and miles and tons and tons of it . . . just up there.

John They'll try to dig in through Moorbanks.

Tom You've been got out before haven't you, John?

John That's right. You'll be all right with me lad. Just press your back against the wall and save your strength.

Alec How long do you reckon?

John We'll just have to wait.

On the Surface:

Seth We'll take that last bit.

Alf Give yourself a rest, Seth.

Seth All of us here has family down there, Alf. We should be allowed to get them out.

Alf You've been there a helluva time. Don't you reckon somebody fresh . . .

Seth We know the seam better than anybody. We should do it. Now come on!

In the kitchen:

Emily "sees" Jackson enter and sing

Song 20a: Hear Your Voice (II)

Jackson   Hear your voice, calling me
         See your eyes, facing me
         Dream of you in my sleep

         But you're not there Emily
         Life with you can never be
         Our two bodies never meet . . .

She also "sees" Harry who says, over Jackson's singing:

Harry Come and see them. Dad and Uncle Isaac and Uncle Seth and everybody. Come on. There's a band and everything.

Finally she "sees" John and sings:

Emily   If I could I would catch them as they fall
        Shield them from the pain,
        And heed their call.

The Seams:

Seth leads the last drive down. A narrow entrance is made. Tom is dragged out first. Alec follows. The sound of a rush

Alec Careful lad, it's coming down again.

Seth John? John.

John It's fallen. Give us a minute.
Seth Hold on to my ankles.
Man Come on lads. Get out.

Black-out

In Emily's kitchen; Emily is sitting in the chair, very still

  May rushes in

May They've got through! They're coming out! He's all right! Mam?
Mam?! Mam!

  John enters and sees May and Emily

Black-out

SCENE 8

The Re-hiring

Seth Terribly raw morning.
John Fresh air and exercise could make a man of you at last.
Seth Wouldn't you like one of those tots of rum they used to give you.
John Well, I'd best be on my way.
Seth We could get you a job on the top you know.
John I know that Seth.
Seth I'll fight for that compensation, never fear.
John I appreciate what you've done.
Seth Medieval in my opinion. Something from the Dark Ages.
John Maybe that's where I belong, Seth. You'll tell May I didn't call in
because it was too early.
Seth I will. She's borne up very well, May.
John She's got her mother's spirit.
Seth I understand, you know. Or I think I do. Why you're doing this. I
don't agree mind: But I think I understand.
John I should've gone back to farm work years ago, Seth. Maybe Emily
would never have gone under if I'd have done that.
Seth You can't blame yourself, John.
John Well, I'd best be on my own now. Thanks for the company.
Seth I'll wait for you.
John I'd as soon be on my own.
Seth Good luck.

Music which has underscored this scene swells into the final chorus

Song 21: Re-hiring: Song of the Hired Men (Reprise)

Each group joins in until all five are being sung simultaneously

All (*in groups*)   Hear us coming O running O singing
                          Over the fields we till

More the work of gods than men
But we'll never no never regret the day
That we put ourselves willing in the
Hiring Ring.
O to be a hired man
O to be a hired man
O to be a hired man ... (*cont.*)

O to be a hired man
O to be a hired man
Men of stone, your wives at home,
Your future's in our hands ... (*cont.*)

Show us your luck pennies will you, O
Show your intentions are that true:
Show us your luck pennies will you, O
Knowing we'll take any that's true ... (*cont.*)

O, listen to our passionate cheers
O, listen to our fearless young cheers ... (*cont.*)
If you lived our lives you'd be the same
In your hearts too would burn such a flame ...

All   If you lived our lives you'd be the same
In your hearts too would burn such a flame.

Chorus   ... O to be a hired man!

Farmer Are you for hire?

John Yes, I'm for hire.

CURTAIN

FURNITURE AND PROPERTY LIST

Only essential props are listed below; further dressing may be added as facilities permit and at the discretion of the director.

ACT I

SCENE 1

Off stage: Whippet **(Seth)**
Jug of beer, glasses **(Landlady)**
Cottage furniture—chairs, table, etc. **(John** and **Emily)**

Personal: **Pennington:** coin
Seth: paper
Isaac: coins
Jackson: coins

SCENE 2

On stage: *In cottage:*
Range with fire
Table
Chairs
Other dressing as required

In work area:
Box with food **(Pennington)**

SCENE 3

Set: Basket and sheets in cottage

Personal: **Jackson:** cigarettes, matches

SCENE 4

Set: Apple pie on cottage table

Off stage: Bag **(Issac)**

Personal: **Isaac:** pipe, matches

SCENE 5

Set: Supper laid out on cottage table

SCENE 6

No props required

ACT II

SCENE 1

Off stage: 3 dead rabbits, gun **(Jackson)**

Personal: **Jackson:** tobacco, papers, matches

SCENE 2

On stage: *In cottage kitchen* (NB. This is a different cottage from the one in Act I):
Table
Chairs
Armchairs
Sideboard or cupboard. *In or on it:* plates, cutlery, food, etc.
Range with fire

Off stage: Pie **(Emily)**

SCENE 3

No props required

SCENE 4

Strike: *In cottage:*
Plates, food, etc. from table

Set: Suitcase, **John**'s belongings
Bag of sweets in vase on sideboard
Piece of brown paper

Personal: **Emily:** piece of heather
Soldiers: cases

SCENE 5

Set: *In cottage:*
Letters, paper, pen for **Emily**

Personal: **Soldiers:** weapons
Jackson: piece of wood

SCENE 6

Set: Camera for **Photographer**
Pie for **Isaac**

Personal: **Seth:** watch

Scene 7

Set: *In cottage:*
                Food for **Emily**
                John's scarf, cap and tin
                Photograph in sideboard

Scene 8

No props required

LIGHTING PLOT

Property fittings required: *nil*

Various simple interior and exterior settings

ACT I SCENE 1

To open: General exterior lighting

Cue 1   As **Emily** and **John** go to the cottage   (Page 8)
         Bring up lights on cottage

Cue 2   **John:** "We've started out."   (Page 9)
         Black-out

ACT I SCENE 2

To open: General exterior lighting; lighting in cottage

Cue 3   At end of Song 5   (Page 11)
         Black-out

ACT I SCENE 3

To open: General exterior lighting; lighting in cottage

Cue 4   **Jackson** stays and watches as **Emily** moves into the house   (Page 13)
         Black-out

ACT I SCENE 4

To open: General exterior lighting; lighting in cottage

Cue 5   **All** (*singing*): "You have—to—pay!—Ha!"   (Page 17)
         Black-out

ACT I SCENE 5

To open: Lighting in cottage; general exterior lighting

Cue 6   At end of Song 9   (Page 21)
         Black-out

ACT I SCENE 6

To open: General exterior lighting

Cue 7   **Isaac:** "... the plagues of Egypt."   (Page 23)
         Dim lighting on "pub"

Cue 8   **Emily:** "Don't go."   (Page 24)
          Increase lighting in "pub"

ACT II Scene 1

To open: General exterior lighting

Cue 9   **Jackson** rolls up a cigarette   (Page 30)
          Fade to Black-out

ACT II Scene 2

To open: Lighting in cottage

Cue 10   At end of Song 15   (Page 34)
          Black-out

ACT II Scene 3

To open: Lighting in cottage

Cue 11   At end of Song 16   (Page 36)
          Black-out

ACT II Scene 4

To open: Lighting on cottage; general exterior lighting

Cue 12   At end of Song 17   (Page 38)
          Fade to Black-out

ACT II Scene 5

To open: Lighting on **Soldiers**; lighting in cottage

Cue 13   **John:** "... now that it's all over."   (Page 43)
          Black-out

ACT II Scene 6

To open: General exterior lighting

Cue 14   At end of Song 20   (Page 47)
          Black-out

ACT II Scene 7

To open: Lighting in cottage; lighting in pit

Cue 15   **John:** " ... just edge back ..."   (Page 48)
          Black-out

Cue 16   When ready   (Page 48)
          Bring up lights on pit surface area and cottage

Cue 17   **Emily:** "... you see. Please."   (Page 48)
          Bring up lights in pit

Cue 18   **Man:** "Come on lads. Get out."   (Page 50)
            Black-out

Cue 19   When ready   (Page 50)
            Bring up lights in cottage

Cue 20   **John** enters and sees **May** and **Emily**   (Page 50)
            Black-out

ACT II Scene 8

To open: General exterior lighting

No cues

EFFECTS PLOT

ACT I

No cues

ACT II

Cue 1	As Scene 1 opens *Sound of birds, then a shot*	(Page 28)
Cue 2	As Scene 5 opens *Gunfire—continue intermittently throughout scene*	(Page 38)
Cue 3	**John:** ". . . another go at her." *First murmurings of the rush*	(Page 48)
Cue 4	**John:** "Sssh." *Low distant rumble*	(Page 48)
Cue 5	Black-out *Klaxon sounds*	(Page 48)
Cue 6	**Tom** is dragged out, **Alec** follows *Sound of a rush*	(Page 49)

MADE AND PRINTED IN GREAT BRITAIN BY
LATIMER TREND & COMPANY LTD PLYMOUTH

MADE IN ENGLAND